For Steen and his love for children's books.
May this one nurture the seed of poetry to grow into flowers of the heart-mind.
— *Esperanza Ramirez-Christensen*

For Lydia and Jun
—*Tracy Gallup*

Note

These poems appear in translation, in original Japanese, and in Romaji. You'll note that the Romaji shows the classic 5-7-5 syllable format for which haiku poetry is famous. Because each language has its own sound system, translations have always varied in syllable count, and may or may not include punctuation, but they strive to be true to the tone and meaning of the original poem.

My First Book of
Haiku Poems

A Picture, a Poem and a Dream

Classic Poems by Japanese Haiku Masters

translated by Esperanza Ramirez-Christensen
illustrated by Tracy Gallup

TUTTLE Publishing

Tokyo | Rutland, Vermont | Singapore

Quick, into the hazy sky!

quickly, quickly—

the bird set free.   —Issa

とくかすめ

とくとくかすめ

放ち鳥   一茶

Toku kasume

toku toku kasume

hanachi-dori   —Issa

In this poem, someone has released a bird from the cage and bids it fly swiftly away until it vanishes in the hazy spring sky. That way, it can't be caught again. But in the picture, the bird seems to have flown from a cage in a *painting*. How did this happen? Think, what does it mean to be free like the bird, and free to imagine?

And the red moon—
to whom does that belong,
children?　　　　　　—Issa

赤い月

これは誰のじゃ

子供たち　　　　　　一茶

Akai tsuki

kore wa tare no ja

kodomo tachi　　　　—*Issa*

How would you answer the poet's question? Does the moon belong to anyone? Does it belong to everyone? What about the sea, the clouds, and the stars and poppy flower in the picture? How do you feel when you spend a lot of time looking at nature? Do you feel connected to everything and everyone? How would you describe that feeling?

On a journey, I'd have

as my companion on the road,

a butterfly.   —Shiki

道づれは

胡蝶をたのむ

旅路かな   — 子規

Michizure wa

kochō wo tanomu

tabiji kana   —Shiki

In the picture, the mom and baby are on a journey to the time when the baby will come into the world. Together they are getting ready for all the big adventures life will hold for them. Butterflies go on a journey when they are born too, don't they? Maybe that's why a butterfly makes a good traveling companion for a journey like this one. It's good to be with someone who understands.

For the poet Shiki the butterfly is a very understanding companion. It flutters alongside so he does not get lonely, stopping here and there to enjoy the beauty of the flowers instead of hurrying to arrive somewhere. Because often the journey is just as important as the arrival, isn't it?

Rarely someone passes,

a withered leaf suddenly adrift,

here, there.　　　　　　　　—Issa

人ちらり

木の葉もちらり

ほらり哉　　　　　　　　一茶

Hito chirari

konoha mo chirari

horari kana　　　　　　—Issa

Withered leaves are what happens in the fall, when the air turns cold and the days feel short. But what happens to fallen acorns when spring comes? Can you imagine the tree that grows from the acorn? So many wonderful things in nature start out very small and have to fall to the ground in order to grow, but the things that come from them are like little worlds, like the one in this picture.

It crawls two or three feet,

then the day is done

for the mud-snail.   —Gomei

二三尺這

うて田螺の

日暮れけり   — 五明

Nisanjaku

haute tanishi no

higurekeri   —Gomei

Some of us just move slower than others. A road that is very short for you is very long for a snail or a turtle. Time passes differently for different beings, including us. How long does it take for wild grass to bear a flower? For leaves to sprout, wither and fall? For the girl to grow too big to ride the turtle? And yet all of these beings that move and grow at different paces live side by side and share the same space.

"Here, come here," I call,

but the fireflies

blithely go their way.   —Onitsura

来い来いと

いへど蛍が

飛んで行く   ― 鬼貫

Koi koi to

iedo hotaru ga

tondeyuku   —*Onitsura*

The haiku and the picture are both about fireflies, but in the picture, it's the imagination that has its way. Have you ever wanted to catch fireflies on a summer night? Then you can imagine how nice it would be if they were unable to fly away, just for a little while, so you can enjoy their flickering lights and share their space. Just you, the night sky and the fireflies, until the jar is opened and out they fly.

The colors of

the dawning sky—a change to

a whole new garment.　　　　　—Issa

曙の

空色衣

かへにけり　　　　　一茶

Akebono no

sora iro koromo

kaenikeri　　　　　—*Issa*

When night becomes day or winter becomes spring, does it ever seem to you that nature is changing its clothes, the same way we change ours? In Issa's day, Japanese people celebrated the coming of summer by putting on new white garments. In this picture, the girl's white nightgown reflects the rose and gold colors of the sky when the sun comes up and night becomes morning. It's as if both she and nature are wearing a "whole new garment."

The year's first dream—
a secret I spoke to no one,
smiling to myself.   —Shōu

初夢や
秘めて語らず
一人笑む   — 松宇

Hatsuyume ya
himete katarazu
hitori emu   —*Shōu*

In some countries, like Japan, it's believed that the first dream of the New Year is important because it tells you what the year holds for you. This boy's dream was a happy one. Why do you think he would he want to keep it a secret? Do you have any happy secrets? Do you have any dreams that go on in your imagination after you wake up?

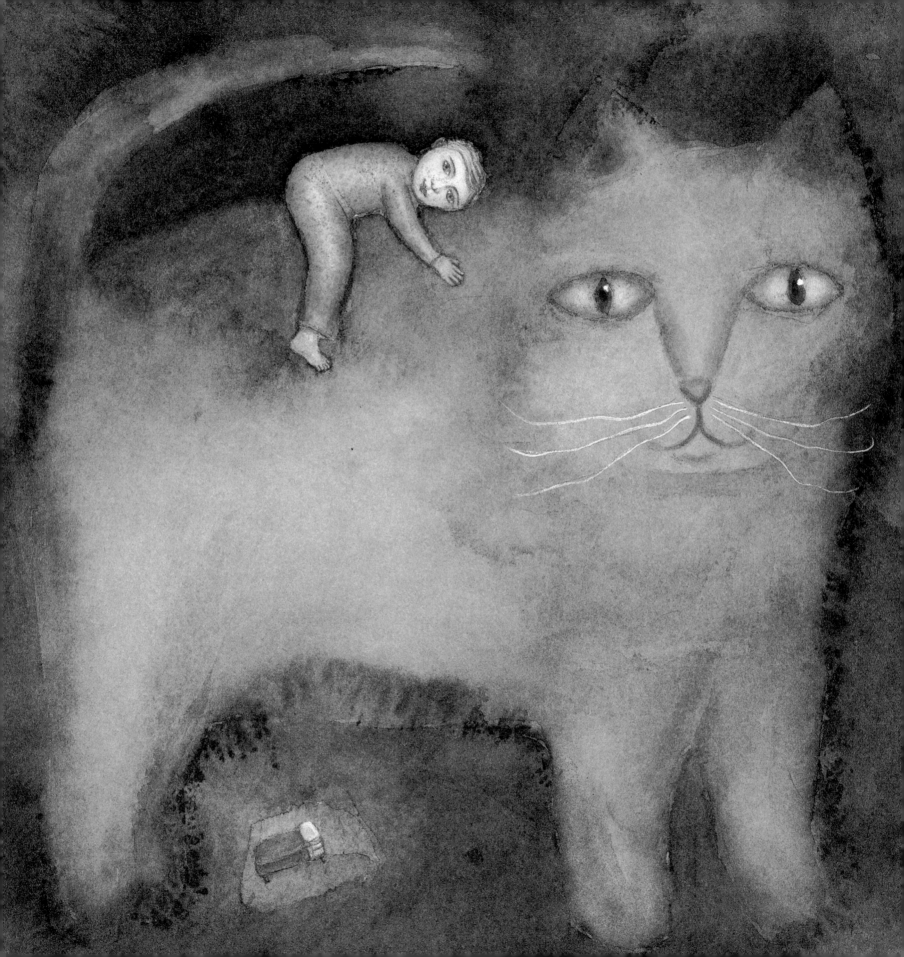

When I looked back,

the one I just met on the road

vanished in the mist.   —Shiki

顧みれば

行き会ひし人

霞みけり   — 子規

Kaerimireba

yukiaishi hito

kasumikeri   *--Shiki*

In this haiku, there is a feeling of mystery and maybe also of loneliness. The girl's companion has gone his own way. Sometimes journeys are like that—we meet new people, but we part company. Do you think the fox is that lost companion? Or do you think the fox is a companion the girl will soon meet, a friend who might share the road with her all the way?

"Get me that moon!"

says the child,

in tears.   —Issa

あの月を

とってくれろと

泣く子哉   一茶

Ano tsuki wo

tottekurero to

naku ko kana   *—Issa*

Do you know the saying, "like crying for the moon"? It means that sometimes the things we want most are things that are beyond our reach. But in the picture, the boy gets his wish, even if it's only in his imagination. How happy he looks with the moon in his hands, flying across the night sky!

A distant sail

under the burning sky—

a sail in my heart.   —Seishi

炎天の

遠き帆やわが

心の帆   — 誓子

　　　＼

Enten no

tōki ho ya waga

kokoro no ho   —Seishi

Why do you think the poet likens a sail on the sea to a sail in his heart? Is the boat carrying away someone he loves? Is the sail in his heart a wish to go to other places and be with people he misses? Or maybe the sail in his heart is a longing for freedom. Sometimes the things we see remind us of other things—people we love, places we want to visit and things we want to do. In the picture, the sea and the sail are all that the eye is seeing. What thoughts do you think may be going on behind the eye?

Just being alive,

the poppy flower

and I.   —Issa

生きてゐる

ばかりぞわれと

けしの花   一茶

Ikiteiru

bakari zo ware to

keshi no hana   —Issa

This poem and picture are about celebrating the joy of the moment, about finding happiness in just being here. It also reminds us that we can't really appreciate the world until we learn to appreciate the little things in it—like a poppy. Looking at this picture, do you think that the poppy is as big as the girl, or that the girl is as small as the poppy?

It seems to like

being pillowed on my arm—

the hazy moon.   —Buson

手枕に

身を愛すなり

朧月   — 蕪村

Tamakura ni

mi wo aisunari

oborozuki   —*Buson*

Did you ever rest your head on the arm of someone you love? In this haiku, moonlight is resting on the poet's arm, like the head of a loved one, happy and content to be resting there. In the picture, it's as if the moon really likes the girl, lighting up her long hair and flower-patterned pajamas in the dark.

Along the rocky shore,

sighing, the waves break,

sighing.   —Issa

磯ぎはに

ざぶりざぶりと

波打ちて   一茶

Isogiwa ni

zaburi-zaburi to

nami uchite   —Issa

Did anyone ever tell you that if you hold a conch shell to your ear, you can hear the sound of the ocean? In this haiku, the poet uses "sighing" to describe the sound of the waves rolling on the shore. Sometimes, when we listen to waves or creeks or fountains, it's like the water is sighing or laughing or singing. And when we are listening very carefully, it can feel as if we are all alone with those wonderful sounds. In the picture, being inside the shell is like being alone with the ocean's sighs.

It looked too heavy,

the water bird,

it floated off anyway. —Onitsura

水鳥の

重たく見えて

浮きにけり   — 鬼貫

Mizudori no

omotaku miete

ukinikeri   —Onitsura

A water bird is made for water. That's why it can float even when it seems too heavy. The bird understands the water, and the water understands the bird. The world is put together in a wonderful way, even though we may not understand everything about it. We are put together in a wonderful way too, and each of us is unique.

Clouds now and then

give them a chance to rest—

moon-viewing.　　　　—Bashō

雲をりをり

人を休むる

月見哉　　　　　— 芭蕉

Kumo ori ori

hito o yasumuru

tsukimi kana　　　　—*Bashō*

In Japan, the full moon of the fall season is thought to be the most beautiful of all the year, and people come together to view it until late in the night. Here Bashō jokes that the people can give their craning necks a break when clouds hide the moon. He uses humor to tell us how much people are willing to endure, to gaze at this perfect moon. In the picture, the girl takes her joy and her imagination even further. She dreams she has been carried to the moon itself. She and the moon are flying on a cloud across the sky. How far will your imagination take you?

The morning breeze—

and skylarks all together soaring

in a perfect line.　　　—Ryōta

朝風や

ただ一筋に

揚雲雀　　　　　-- 蓼太

Asakaze ya

tada hitosuji ni

agehibari　　　　—*Ryōta*

Although the picture does not show the birds flying in a single line, it does show them working together. They are so focused on helping each other ride the wind safely, it's as if they form one big bird. What can we learn from the birds and other creatures of nature?

Whose lamp yet burns,
unsleeping—this night of
cold driving rain?   —Ryōta

何人の
寝ぬ灯ぞ
小夜時雨　　　　　— 蓼太

Nanibito no
nenu tomoshibi zo
sayoshigure　　　　　*—Ryōta*

Sometimes, we all feel wide awake long after we should be asleep. What keeps us up, do you think?
Sometimes we are too excited or wound up to sleep. Other times, we may be worried or frightened or sad.
Why do you think the girl in this picture is awake, and what is she thinking as she watches the moths flying
in the rain outside her window?

Getting warm and snug

enfolded within the snow—

my domicile.   —Issa

ほちほちと

雪にくるまる

在所哉   一茶

Hochi-hochi to

yuki ni kurumaru

zaisho kana   —*Issa*

Do you feel more cozy inside when there's snow outside? "Domicile" is a fancy way of saying "house." By choosing that word, Issa was suggesting that his little home was like a castle to him, and he was its lord. Warm and snug in his house, he watches the cold, beautiful snow falling outside. His house is snug in this snow, just as he is snug in his little house. In this picture, a boy and bunny are snuggled together, warm and peaceful. Their little house keeps them safe, but lets them feel a part of all the beautiful wintry world around them.

As an added delight,

how cool blows the breeze--

sleeping among the stars.　—Issa

御馳走に

涼風吹くや

星の閨　　　　　　　一茶

Gochisō ni/

suzukaze fuku ya

hoshi no neya　　　　*—Issa*

The poem suggests that the poet has just had a lovely evening, maybe with a friend. Afterwards, he is dozing outdoors, enjoying the light summer breeze, almost like a sweet dessert after a wonderful dinner. Maybe the poem is his way of saying "thank you" to his friend. In the picture, the children are enjoying the feeling of sleeping among the stars, floating in the sky with their dreams and their cat, or lying awake, chatting together in the fresh night breeze. And maybe they are thankful too.

A Haiku by You

Look at all the elements in this picture: a girl, a bird flying by, a book, a doll, a ball, a dark room with a splash of light coming through the open door. What do they make you think of? How do they make you feel? What kind of haiku can you write using some or all of the things you see here? Why not write one on this page? See if you can write it in three lines, with five syllables in the first and third lines, and seven in the second line, just like the original Japanese haiku were written.

Many different things influence writers, poets and artists. The poets in this book came from different parts of Japan and were born generations and sometimes even centuries apart from one another. They came from different social classes, whether samurai, farmer, or tradesman. Some lived during times of war. Most traveled to different parts of Japan. All of the things in these poets' lives shaped their view of the world, and that is something that has always been true of all of us.

Earlier generations of poets influenced later generations, and poets in the same generation also influenced one another. They also wrote together through a form of poetry called *haikai no renga* or simply, *haikai*. In this form, a group of poets write verses that link to each other. It is part game, part group effort. The end result is one long poem. The form of poetry called *haiku* was at first only the opening verse of these longer poems. Later, it became a form in its own right.

Some of these poets also wrote diaries of their lives and travels, essays, and the other form of classical poem called *tanka*. There is so much to learn about each of them! Here is just a little bit about the lives and work of the poets in this book.

Matsuo Bashō (1644–1694) is the best known of all the poets whose haiku appear in this book, and most of these poets were influenced by his work. He lived during a time called the Edo period (1600-1868). In these years, Japan largely closed itself off from visitors and travel abroad, and depended on itself for everything, including poetry. It was a time when writers and artists were inspired by the beauty of their own country— its nature, and its people.
Bashō is famous for composing linked verses with his followers and friends. It is a form of poetry he especially loved. He is also famous for making long walking journeys through the countryside while composing poems, and for long periods of remaining alone. Between the two, he had the chance to observe nature and spend time in quiet thought. Those two things came together to help him write some of the best haiku in Japanese history.

Yosa Buson (1716–1784) was another great poet of the Edo period. He was famous for being both a painter and a poet, and he used his poems to describe the things he saw. He loved the art and poetry of China. He also loved the work of Bashō, and drew illustrations for Bashō's best-known travel journal. After traveling in many parts of Japan to develop his arts, he settled down to live and teach in the city of Kyoto.

Kikkawa Gomei (1731–1803) lived in the time of Buson and Issa. Though he is not as well known today as other poets in this book, he was popular during his time, becoming known as one of the "four deva kings [of *haikai*]" in the North, and is said to have been a great teacher of poetry. His poems are included in Issa's verse collection, *Farewell Hat*, from 1798.

Kobayashi Issa (1763-1828) wrote many of the poems that appear in this book. He, Bashō and Buson are known as the three great leaders of *haikai*. He suffered many losses in the first half of his life, and his sadness is reflected in some of his verses. Issa wrote over twenty thousand poems. While some of them are indeed sad, others are about the pleasures of nature and of observing children. Issa, whose name means "cup of tea," is known for his verses about small things like fireflies and frogs and flowers. His poems have been popular through the years because of their gentleness, their humor and the simple way that they capture everyday things and moments.

Uejima Onitsura (1661–1738) showed a talent for poetry even when he was a child. It is said that he wrote the verse "Here, come here, I call/ but the fireflies/ blithely go their way," included in this book, when he was only eight. Although born to a wealthy family, he devoted himself to poetry and philosophy. He believed that haiku should reflect everyday things and ordinary life—that it should be sincere and truthful, and speak to our hearts. Later in his life, Onitsura focused on his practice of Zen Buddhism.

Ōshima Ryōta (1718-1787) was one of Bashō's greatest followers. He imitated Bashō's travels and collected the poems Bashō had written during his long journey though the North. A poet of great energy and talent, he is said to have produced some two hundred books of poetry by himself and others, and taught about two thousand students.

Masaoka Shiki (1867-1902) lived in the Meiji era (1868-1926), a time when Japan opened its doors to the world again and quickly learned about Western culture and technology. Shiki felt that Japan's poetic tradition was too simple for a nation that was rapidly changing, and created a new style of haiku called "copying from life"—writing about what one is seeing in the present moment, instead of relying on learning and tradition. Shiki came from a samurai family, and always remained interested his country's politics. He even traveled to China to report on the war. He died young from a long illness, but in his short life he had written some eighteen thousand haiku.

Yamaguchi Seishi (1901-1994) studied law at Tokyo University and worked for a big company. He was known for poems that included elements of modern life, like blast furnaces, trains and sports. His best haiku are about those moments when the natural world meets the world of people and the things they've made. They are poems that bring traditional haiku and its love of nature together with the modern world.

Itō Shōu (1859-1943) was a poet of the Meiji era, and an acquaintance of Shiki, though not as well known. A lot of his work was devoted to writing about haiku, linked verses, and rules for holding writing sessions through the ages. By doing this, and by collecting the writings of other poets, he explained the world of older generations of haiku masters, to preserve their styles and themes for his own and future generations.

To parents and teachers, from the translator

How did this book come about? My neighbor, Tracy Gallup, is a writer and illustrator of children's books, and has an affinity for haiku. She showed me some of her paintings side by side with related haiku poems by Japanese master poets such as Buson, Issa and others in the early modern period and said that she had been keenly struck by how closely the poems expressed or evoked some of the paintings she had done earlier without knowing that the kindred Japanese poems existed. She showed me the pairings that had struck her and, indeed, the mutual resonance between them was striking. She asked me if I would do new translations of the poems in place of the old ones by R. H. Blythe. In the process, I discovered that the nature of the connections between the haiku and Tracy's paintings was very much like the links from one verse to the next in the collective Japanese poetry sequence called *renga*, "linked poetry." In this collaborative genre, each successive verse is composed by a different poet, and although there are rules for composing a sequence, there is no predetermined topic and the verses are all composed on the spot.

Renga is a performance like a jazz session; each poet is harmonizing with the other while at the same time altering the other's composition in the process of shaping his or her own part. This sort of harmonizing transforms rather than repeats. The poet reads the preceding verse and responds to it by continuing the story, by putting it in a different context, creating contrast, intensifying the other's message, carrying the story forward.

The haiku can be read and appreciated on their own, of course, and the same goes for the pictures. But isn't it fascinating to see each one juxtaposed against the other and think what results? To look at the similarities and differences between the two, and sense how they are communicating with one another, even though they were created in vastly different times and places? To see how the dots connect through time, place and culture—is that not a marvelous thing? It is a way of discovering and broadening the imagination from early on, not just through the links between poem and picture; through the minds and hearts that dwell in them, we also see the bigger picture, the universal patterns of relation between human beings and their natural environment, between time and the various motions of plant, animal and human lives that resonate with one another in our world. Everything is connected. Haiku and painting are two simple ways of sharing and celebrating that truth with children.

As you embark on this artistic and poetic adventure with your children, I would like to share with you part of a 1468 renga session among samurai warriors and Buddhist monks about the pleasures of encounter even among strangers amidst the beauty of springtime, and our need for the kind of awareness that poetry and art ignite and express:

1 Here in the shadow of
the trees the first snow patches
have yet to dissolve (Mitsusuke)

2 Yet sweet is the morning dew
as one by one plum blossoms unfurl (Shinkei)

3 Ah, the spring meadows—
even the sleeves of strangers
brushing each other (Norishige)

4 On the bay overhung with haze,
boats seen gliding to and fro (Sōgi)

5 For the man devoid
of feeling, the dimming evening
holds nothing (Sōetsu)

A Word From the Artist

Poets and artists often think alike. Haiku especially is similar to a visual image because it often represents a single moment. Finding poems that align with my paintings has been a revelation. To realize I have shared the same thoughts with people from distant times and places makes me feel like a time traveler. How magical to meet a soul mate through words, with a man like Kobayashi Issa, born 1763 in Japan. In this twenty first century I look at the same moon as he did and imagine ...

Note

Classic haiku, including the ones in this book, have been translated many times by generations of scholars, and each translation is unique, resulting in different interpretations of the poem's meaning. We encourage you to explore books and websites that offer different translations of haiku masters' work. The key to any enduring poem is how it connects with those who read it, and we think you'll find that these poems continue to resonate regardless of when and where they were written, and of how translators have interpreted them over the years.

We hope these poems will be just the beginning of children's exploration of haiku at its roots, and will help foster in them a love of poetry and an appreciation of its power to connect us with nature, with one another and with ourselves.

"Books to Span the East and West"

Tuttle Publishing was founded in 1832 in the small New England town of Rutland, Vermont [USA]. Our core values remain as strong today as they were then—to publish best-in-class books which bring people together one page at a time. In 1948, we established a publishing office in Japan—and Tuttle is now a leader in publishing English-language books about the arts, languages and cultures of Asia. The world has become a much smaller place today and Asia's economic and cultural influence has grown. Yet the need for meaningful dialogue and information about this diverse region has never been greater. Over the past seven decades, Tuttle has published thousands of books on subjects ranging from martial arts and paper crafts to language learning and literature—and our talented authors, illustrators, designers and photographers have won many prestigious awards. We welcome you to explore the wealth of information available on Asia at **www.tuttlepublishing.com**.

Published by Tuttle Publishing, an imprint of Periplus Editions (HK) Ltd.

www.tuttlepublishing.com

The *renga* sequence on page 3 is taken from *Heart's Flower: The Life and Poetry of Shinkei* by Esperanza Ramirez-Christensen (Stanford University Press, 1994) and appears here by permission of the publisher.

Library of Congress Cataloging-in-Publication Data for this title is in progress.

ISBN 978-4-8053-1515-6

Distributed by

North America, Latin America & Europe
Tuttle Publishing
364 Innovation Drive
North Clarendon, VT 05759-9436 U.S.A.
Tel: 1 (802) 773-8930
Fax: 1 (802) 773-6993
info@tuttlepublishing.com
www.tuttlepublishing.com

Japan
Tuttle Publishing
Yaekari Building, 3rd Floor
5-4-12 Osaki
Shinagawa-ku, Tokyo 141 0032
Tel: (81) 3 5437-0171
Fax: (81) 3 5437-0755
sales@tuttle.co.jp
www.tuttle.co.jp

Asia Pacific
Berkeley Books Pte. Ltd.
3 Kallang Sector #04-01/02
Singapore 349278
Tel: (65) 6741-2178
Fax: (65) 6741-2179
inquiries@periplus.com.sg
www.tuttlepublishing.com

First edition
24 23 22 21   10 9 8 7 6 5 4 3   2111VP
Printed in Malaysia